Bud Barkin, Private Eye

JAMES HOWE

ILLUSTRATED BY BRETT HELQUIST

Aladdin Paperbacks
New York London Toronto Sydney

First Aladdin Paperbacks edition May 2004

ALADDIN PAPERBACKS
An imprint of Simon & Schuster
Children's Publishing Division
1230 Avenue of the Americas
New York, NY 10020

Also available in an Atheneum Books for Young Readers hardcover edition.
Designed by Ann Bobco
The text of this book was set in Berkeley.
The illustrations were rendered in acrylics and oils.

Printed in the United States of America
10 9 8 7 6 5 4 3 2 1

The Library of Congress has cataloged the hardcover edition as follows:
Howe, James, 1946–
Bud Barkin, private eye / James Howe; illustrated by Brett Helquist.
p. cm.—(Tales from the House of Bunnicula, #5)
Summary: Howie the wirehaired dachshund tries his paw at writing a new kind of novel, a mystery in which he imagines himself as a private investigator and Delilah as the "mysterious dame."
ISBN 0-689-85632-6 (hc.)
[1. Authorship—Fiction. 2. Dachshunds—Fiction. 3. Dogs—Fiction. 4. Mystery and detective stories. 5. Humorous stories.] I. Helquist, Brett, ill. II. Title. III. Series: Howe, James, 1946–. Tales from the house of Bunnicula, #5.
PZ7 .H83727B 2003
[Fic]—dc21 2002012888
ISBN 0-689-86989-4 (Aladdin pbk.)

The name's Mark Davis. He's a great guy. He'd make a great dog. This book is dedicated to him. With love, happiness, and Thanks with a capital T.

—J. H.

For Mary Jane

—B. H.

HOWIE'S WRITING JOURNAL

Okay, fine. My last book <u>didn't</u> win the Newbony Award. Who cares? My readers liked it, that's all that matters. Now that I've written four books, I get letters from my readers all the time. That is <u>so</u> cool! I got one just the other day from this girl named Krystel, who said I'm her <u>favorite author</u>!

"Dear Howie Monroe," she wrote, "you are my favorite author. I haven't read any of your books, but if I have time someday, maybe I will."

That is *so* cool!

Then this boy named Jayson wrote, "I like your stories. They sure are funny. The only problem is that there aren't any pigs in your stories. Why don't you write about pigs? Don't you like pigs? Other than not having any pigs, I think your stories are good."

I like pigs. Who said I didn't like pigs?

I tried writing a story about a pig once. It was about a pig that was turned into a monster by a mad scientist. It was called Frankenswine. The problem was, it ended up sounding too much like a book Uncle Harold wrote about our rabbit. Uncle Harold said that was okay, that there are lots of books that are kind of like other books. He mentioned a certain book of mine (see Book #3: Howie Monroe and the Doghouse of Doom), but that was different. I don't know why, but it was. The thing is, I don't want to write the same kinds of stories as Uncle Harold.

Except, I wouldn't mind writing a mystery,

even if Uncle Harold has already written some. I mean, lots of authors have written mysteries. Uncle Harold didn't invent them. (At least, I don't think he did. I'll have to ask.)

Uncle Harold says that mysteries are hard to write. He says even though he usually doesn't outline his books first, with mysteries he needs to because mysteries are like puzzles and you have to know where all the pieces fit.

That sounds like way too much work.

I'm going to go take a nap.

HOWIE'S WRITING JOURNAL

Outline for mystery story

I. Mysterious thing happens

II. Detective called in to investigate

III. Detective checks it out

IV. Detective solves the case

I don't know what Uncle Harold is talk-ing about. That wasn't hard at all!

Howie's Writing Journal

I let Uncle Harold read my outline. Well, that was a mistake. He said I need more details.

"Like what?" I asked.

"Like the crime," he told me. "With a mystery, always start with the crime and work backward."

Backward? It's hard enough writing forward!

He said I need to figure out who committed the crime and why they did it, and then I need to make other characters seem suspicious so the reader will think one of <u>them</u> did it instead of the real criminal.

He said something about red herrings, which I didn't understand at all. (I know Uncle Harold has food on the brain, but I didn't think he liked fish.)

He suggested I read some mysteries before trying to write one. That's easy enough to do. Mr. Monroe is a big mystery reader. I'll just sneak into his study after everybody's asleep. I'll read all the mysteries I can get my paws on. If I read enough of them, I'll have all the details I need.

Maybe I'll even have an idea!

Bud Barkin, Private Eye

By Howie Monroe

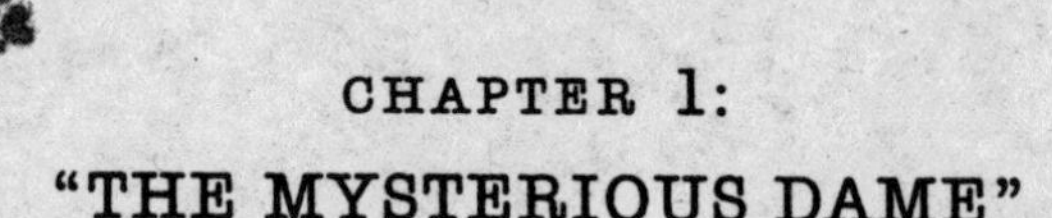

CHAPTER 1: "THE MYSTERIOUS DAME"

I was working late. It was past my bedtime, but I didn't care because twenty out of twenty-four hours is my bedtime. I'm a dog. I'm a detective. The name's Bud Barkin.

The light from the sign outside my window was blinking like a firefly with a bad case of the hiccups. I was used to it. The sign for the Big Slice Pizzeria had been there as long as I

had. I'd just finished off a pepperoni and mushroom pizza—dinner alone, as usual—when I heard a knock on my door. My ears popped up like a couple of prairie dogs.

Who would come knocking on my door at this hour? I was hoping it wasn't Crusty Carmady. I'd just read in that evening's *Chronicle* that Crusty'd been sprung from Sing Sing. It was I that sent him up. His last words to me were, "I'll be gettin' outa here one of these days, Barkin. And when I do, put the water on fer tea 'cause I'll be payin' youse a little visit."

I inched my way across the room to the door. The top half of the door was frosted glass with words painted on it. A shadow fell across BUD BARKIN, PRIVATE EYE.

I held my breath.

"That you, Carmady?" I said.

There was the sound of breathing coming from the other side, but it wasn't Crusty's. I'd recognize his breathing anywhere. It was as raspy as a dull knife scraping across a piece of burnt toast. This breathing was fast and flighty, like a hummingbird with a bad case of the jitters.

I knew right away: The breather was a dame.

I pulled the door open. She toppled into me. One blonde curly ear hid half her face, but I could see right off she was Trouble with a capital T.

"Mr. Barkin," she pleaded, "you gotta help me."

"Do I, sweetheart?" I said. I may have been a private eye who was down on his luck, but I still had a way with words.

The dame was whimpering now. "C-Close the door," she stammered. "I'm being f-followed."

I did like she asked.

"Drink?" I offered, filling the extra water dish I keep handy.

"Don't mind if I do," she said, slurping as noisily as a gang of schoolkids splashing through a puddle at the tail end of a rainy day. I noticed that once she was inside the room, she didn't seem so scared. I smelled a rat and it wasn't pretty. This dame was up to something.

"What's your name, sweetheart?" I asked her.

"Delilah," she told me. "Delilah Gorbish. I

just breezed into town. Haven't been here but seven days and I'm in danger. It's enough to make one weak."

I ignored her clever pun, wishing I'd thought of it myself. "What kind of danger you in, angel face?" I asked.

"The kind that leaves you shaking like a bowl of Jell-O on a stormy sea," she said.

"That's the worst kind," I told her.

She opened her purse and took out a box. "A certain party back home asked me to deliver this to a mutual acquaintance, but he was not at the address I was given. I've tried locating him, but I've had no luck. And now I have the distinct impression that I'm being followed. Somebody wants this box."

"Or they want to make sure it doesn't get to

the party for whom it was intended," I interjected wisely. "What's inside the box, anyway?"

She shook her head. "I don't know. It's sealed shut, and I was instructed not to open it. I was told . . . I was told it was safer for me not to know its contents."

"You're in a pickle, all right."

"So you'll help me? Please, Mr. Barkin, say yes. I'm as frightened as a cockroach when the lights snap on and there's no place to hide."

I didn't know what to think. Maybe she was on the up-and-up. Besides, I needed the dough. The last time I checked under my mattress, the only thing I found was a set of broken-down springs. I'd spent my last dime on a cheap chew bone, and that was two days ago. The pizza I'd had for dinner? Courtesy of the Dumpster in back of the Big Slice.

"It'll cost you," I told her.

"I've got money," she told me back. "Cash money."

"That's the best kind," I said. "Just one thing, sweetheart. If we're going to be working together?"

"Yes?"

"I'll do the similes."

Howie's Writing Journal

This is awesome! I'm pretending to be somebody else! I got the idea from reading some of Mr. Monroe's mysteries. I like being Bud Barkin. He's tough. The only problem is, I don't know how to describe him to my readers. I can't say, "the smart and clever, not to mention adorable me!"

Can I?

I think I'll try another chapter, and then

I'll show what I've written to Uncle Harold.

(I hope my readers won't miss the character of Howie Monroe too much. He was so smart and clever. Not to mention adorable.)

for the count. If I'd been smart, I would have kicked her out of my office then and there. But I've always been a sucker for dames. Especially ones with cash money.

After counting to ten—"one potato, two potato, three potato, four . . ."—I took my paw away from her snout and went to investigate the object lying in the heap of broken glass.

It was a teakettle.

"Crusty Carmady," I muttered.

"Crusty wouldn't have tossed a teakettle. He's not that refined," Delilah Gorbish said.

I turned my piercing and keenly perceptive eyes on her. "What'd you say?" I asked in a tough and manly way.

"N-Nothing," she stammered, her face as

confused and twisted as a pretzel doing yoga.

"What do you know about Carmady?" I snapped. "Don't play the innocent with me now, precious. I'm on to your tricks."

"Oh, really? You ever seen me fetch?"

"Leave the jokes to me," I told her. "Now tell me what you know about Crusty Carmady."

Her eyes got all misty. I sensed we were heading for a flashback.

"We sang in the church choir together," she told me. "This was back in Iowa before . . . before Crusty went bad. He wasn't called Crusty then. He was Chris. Or Cris. Maybe it was Kris. I can never remember. Anyway, he fell in with the wrong crowd, and one day he left town and never looked back."

"So you went looking for *him*," I said. "He's the one you're supposed to deliver that box to, isn't he?"

She looked me over like I was a used car she was thinking of buying if the price was right. I half expected her to kick my tires. "Nothing gets by you, does it, Mr. Barkin?" she said coolly. "Not only are you impossibly handsome in a cute and puppyish sort of way, but you're smart and intelligent, too. And as sensitive as . . ."

She stopped, remembering that I was the one doing the similes.

"As a finely tuned concert piano." I finished the sentence for her.

"We could make some beautiful music together," she said with a sigh, letting an ear flop back over her face so that only one eye was showing.

"Maybe later," I said, fighting the impulse to restring my harp and play her a tune or two. "Right now we've got a killer to catch."

"Crusty may no longer be a choirboy," said Delilah, shaking her ears out, "but he's no killer."

"Details, details," I muttered. "He's still trouble."

"With a capital T," Delilah said. "Are you going after him?"

"You bet I am, lamb chop," I told her. "You stay here and make yourself useful. Do you know anything about fixing windows?"

She reached into her purse and took out a tube of caulking. "You leave that window to me," she said. "I'm not a former straight-A student of Miss Lucille's Dance and Window Glazing Academy for nothing."

I cracked a smile. "You're all right," I told her.

She cracked a smile right back at me. "Hadn't you better hurry? Crusty's waiting for you. I mean, uh, you don't want him to get away."

My gut got as tight as a pair of all-cotton briefs after they'd been dried on high when the directions clearly stated tumble dry *low*. Was it something she said?

Or was it time to stop eating pizza out of a Dumpster?

Howie's Writing Journal

Uncle Harold read what I wrote so far and said, "Howie, this may be your best writing yet!"

Wow! Maybe this book will win the Newbony Award! Or at least get better reviews than my last one. Obedience School Library Journal said about Screaming Mummies of the Pharaoh's Tomb II:

> Howie Monroe and Delilah Gorbish can't seem to make up their minds in this confused and meandering story

about orphans, time travel, and mummies in need of therapy. If your shelf space is limited, stick with M. T. Graves's original and now classic *Screaming Mummies of the Pharaoh's Tomb.*

Delilah was so depressed after reading that review, she wouldn't play Rip-the-Rag for a week. Hey, maybe this new book will cheer her up! I'll bet she'll love how I made her a mysterious dame. I'll show it to her later.

Let's see, what else did Uncle Harold say? He liked that I was writing in the first person (that's what it's called when you write as "I" instead of "he" or "she"), and he thought I was doing a good job with the character of Bud Barkin but that I didn't need so many adjectives. Poor Uncle Harold. He can't stop talking about adjectives. I wonder if he wasn't praised enough as a puppy.

CHAPTER 3:
"A RED HERRING"

I spent the night scouring the city for Crusty Carmady, but he wasn't in any of his usual haunts. Dog tired, I headed back to the office just before dawn.

The door was ajar. (Actually, it was still a door. "Ajar" means it was slightly open.)

Delilah had replaced the window. I'd never seen caulking like it. What a pro. She'd even repainted the sign:

BUD BARKIN

PRIVATE Ehelp

Being smart and intelligent, not to mention bright and well educated, I noticed right off the bat that the word "eye" was misspelled. Maybe they didn't teach spelling at that fancy school Delilah had gone to. Or maybe she was trying to tell me something.

My brain was spared the trouble of trying to figure it all out by the sound of whistling coming from the other side of the door.

"Is that you, toots?" I called out.

If it was Delilah, she just kept on whistling.

Tired as I was, I was awake enough to notice that that didn't sound like a dame's whistle. I was thinking: *Carmady*.

I tried putting my paw in my trench coat

pocket to pretend I had a gun when I remembered I didn't have a trench coat or a pocket. That's what's known in the detective game as a complication. So I just pushed the door open and called out, "Don't make a move!"

The dame was as missing as a first grader's front tooth.

In the blinking light of the Big Slice Pizzeria, I could make out what was whistling. It was the teakettle! Call it instinct or call it the fact that all of a sudden I made sense out of the misspelled word on my door, but the whole picture fell into place. While I'd been out looking for Carmady, Carmady had been here! And it looked like he'd left with the best caulker and sign painter I'd ever known. All she'd had time to do was scrawl out the word "help" on the window.

I had to find her.

But what if it was a trap? What if Delilah and Crusty were setting me up for a big fall? What if they were the cats and I was the mouse? What if they were the mice and I was the cheese? What if they were the cheese and I was . . . something easily threatened by cheese?

I shook the questions out of my head. Asking questions right now was as useless as boiling water for tea when the last tea bag had been double dipped three weeks before. I turned the heat off under the kettle.

Lucky for me I was standing where I was, because just then an object came crashing through the newly glazed plateglass window. My first thought was, *Oh, boy, Delilah isn't going to like this!* My second thought was, *Somebody's out to get me!*

I made my way across the room as cautiously as a caterpillar crossing the interstate.

Whatever it was, was wrapped in a newspaper. The story about Carmady being released from the slammer hit my eyes just as the paper's contents hit my nostrils. I knew what was in there even before I opened it.

A red herring.

And that could only mean one thing: the Big Fish!

Howie's Writing Journal

The Big Fish? What is that supposed to mean?!

I hate when this happens. I'm just writing along, minding my own business, when all of a sudden I have no idea what I'm writing about.

Maybe Uncle Harold was right—maybe I should have put more details in my outline. If I ask him for help, that's probably what he'll tell me. I hate it when he says, "I told you so."

I could ask Delilah for help instead. She and I wrote a book together (see Book #4: <u>Screaming Mummies of the Pharaoh's Tomb II</u>) (do <u>not</u> pay any attention to that stinko review in <u>Obedience School Library Journal</u>), so she knows a thing or two about writing. Maybe she'll have some ideas about what the Big Fish could mean.

Howie's Writing Journal

Great. Delilah didn't even want to talk about the Big Fish. All she could talk about was her character. She said, "Howie, you've turned me into a stereotype again."

I don't know how she knows words like that. I think it's from hanging around her owner, Amber Faye Gorbish, who has pretty strong opinions about things.

"What do you mean?" I asked.

"You've made me this dumb, helpless blonde, and there you are being the big hero!"

"Well, I may be the hero, but there's more to Delilah than meets the eye," I pointed out. "At least, there will be when I figure out what it is."

Delilah scowled. "Think of all the work we did developing characters in <u>our</u> book. Didn't you learn anything from writing a book together?"

"Sure," I said. What I'd learned was that we should never write a book together again. Ever.

Delilah shook her head. "Well, I'm disappointed in you, that's all I have to say." And she walked away.

I'm beginning to think maybe I shouldn't use my friends in my stories.

I was on my way to asking Pop (that's what I call this really cool cat we live with, whose real name is Chester) when I bumped into Uncle Harold.

"How's the writing going?" he asked.

I showed him what I'd written and asked him if he knew what the Big Fish could mean.

He said, "Did you outline?"

I changed the subject. "I was trying to write about a red herring."

He explained, "Howie, a red herring doesn't

have to have anything to do with a real fish. There _is_ a real fish called a red herring, but in a mystery a 'red herring' is a term meaning something you put in the story to lead your readers in the wrong direction. It might be something that would make them suspect the wrong character of committing the crime, for instance."

"Character!" I said. "That's it! I'll make the Big Fish a character! Gee, Uncle Harold, thanks!"

"You're welcome," he said. He shook his head just the way Delilah had.

I wonder if they have fleas.

CHAPTER 4:
"THE BIG FISH"

It had been a couple of years since I'd seen the Big Fish, but I knew where to find him. He was the kind of criminal who liked to keep what's known in the detective game as a "low profile," meaning he didn't want to take any chances on being seen in the wrong place at the wrong time. Besides, I had it on good authority that he never went out because he was addicted to the Home Shopping Network. It was a costly habit. To support it, he employed a gang of low-life types to commit petty robberies. If they got caught, they were warned not to sing.

Word had it that Crusty Carmady sang.

The office of the Big Fish's cover operation, Small Pond Enterprises, was right where I'd remembered it: on the corner of Thirty-third and Third.

I got to the door, looked to my left, looked to my right, and was all set to ring the bell when I realized I couldn't remember the code. Was it three long rings and two short, or two short rings and three long? I tried three long and two short. A voice on the other side of the door said, "Go away, nobody's here."

Rats.

Being the sort who isn't easily discouraged, I decided to give it another try.

Two long and three short.

A tiny window slid open. A pair of eyes as cold and hard as an ice-cream truck stuck in a blizzard stared out at me.

"What's the password?" a voice growled.

That one was easy, so long as they hadn't changed it since the last time I paid the Big Fish a visit. "I see London, I see France, I can see your underpants."

Bingo. The window shut and the door opened.

One of the Big Fish's goons ushered me into the inner sanctum. The Big Fish sat in a big chair, his eyes reflecting the oxidized two-tone link bracelet with old-world appeal currently being offered on the big-screen TV in front of him.

The Big Fish wasn't really a fish. He just smelled like one. (He *was* big, however.)

"You got my calling card," he said, his bloodshot eyes never moving from the screen.

"The red herring?"

"Precisely. Sit, Barkin."

I sat. I may have been an obedience school dropout, but I'd learned a thing or two in my time.

"May I offer you a chew bone? I had them flown in from the Pet Channel." The Big Fish was a class act. I accepted the chew bone and waited to hear what he had to say.

"I got a proposition to make," he told me. One of his hefty paws was on the phone, poised to call in his order for the fourteen-

carat gold link necklace dripping with zircons that had replaced the sold-out oxidized two-tone link bracelet.

"I'm all ears," I said, which was, in fact, an anatomical impossibility. I still had only two ears.

"Mr. Crusty Carmady has something that belongs to me. I want you to get it back."

"Me?" I said.

It took the Big Fish a while to answer. Either he was distracted by the set of nesting canisters currently being offered at the ridiculously low price of $12.95 or he was giving my question serious thought.

"You," he said at last.

I slid the chew bone around to one side of my mouth so I wouldn't trip all over the big speech coming next. "But what can *I* do?" I asked him. "I'm only one small dachshund in a world gone mad, one tiny voice in a sea of voices, one pebble in a field of boulders, one itsy-bitsy minnow in a school of sharks!"

"Save that kind of talk for your other books," he snapped. "You and I both know you're the only one for this job. Now get out there and do it."

"But I don't know what I'm looking for," I pointed out.

"Come on, Barkin, there hasn't even been a crime in this story yet. If I tell you what you're looking for, there'll be no mystery at all."

"Fair enough. But can't I at least have a clue?"

"Fine. I'll tell you this: She's—"

That's all I got out of him, because just then an object came crashing through the window and conked the Big Fish on the noggin. He slumped forward, dropping his phone to the floor as a voice on the other end repeated, "Will that be Visa or MasterCard? Visa or MasterCard?"

I waved off the Big Fish's goons so I could move in and get a closer look at what had done him in.

It was a book.

"I warned da boss about dem bookmobiles," the goon to my left said.

"This is no book from a bookmobile," I replied confidently. "This is a carefully planted clue. Just look at the title."

I held up the book for everyone to see: *Songs for Sopranos*.

There was only one soprano in this story that I knew of. Her name was *Delilah Gorbish!*

CHAPTER 5:
"A CUP OF JAVA"

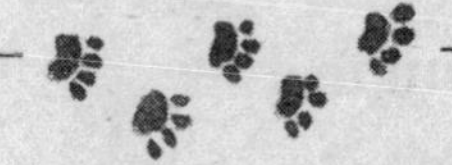

When you've been playing the detective game as long as I have, you know a few things, like never trust a stranger and always put your pants on one leg at a time. But then there are times when something comes out of nowhere like a bad rash and it makes no sense and all you know is what you don't know and you wish you could call it a day and start all over again in the morning. Delilah Gorbish was like that.

(NOTE to the real Delilah: You are *not* like a bad rash. Remember that this is a story and therefore full of fine literary writing that has nothing to do with you or anything else that's real.)

The thing I couldn't figure was whether Delilah was innocent and needed to be rescued or whether she and Carmady were in cahoots. I decided to blow some of the cash money Delilah had advanced me for a cup of java and review what I knew.

The waitress at Java Hut was named Millie. She had a look in her eye that spelled Trouble with a capital T. But that's another story.

So, I thought, watching the steam rise from my double espresso double skim mocha latte, *what do I know? Well, I know all the state capitals east of the Mississippi and I know how to spell*

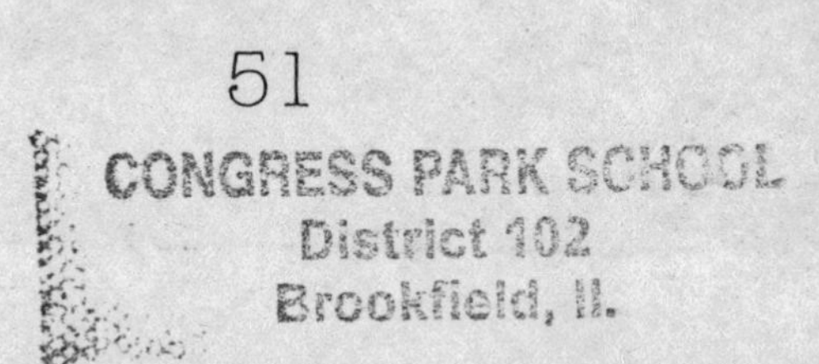

"Mississippi," but a fat lot of good that information will do me now.

I didn't have a clue what I was supposed to be finding for the Big Fish.

But wait! I *did* have a clue. The Big Fish had started to say something before he took a nosedive onto his authentically handcrafted Persian carpet with oxidized two-tone fringe. He'd said, "She's—"

Whatever he wanted me to find for him was of the female persuasion. Well, there was only one thing of the female persuasion in this story that I knew of, besides Millie, and like I said, that's another story.

Whether she was a dangerous dame or a damsel in distress, it was time to find Delilah Gorbish!

CHAPTER 6:
"A GUY NAMED EDDIE"

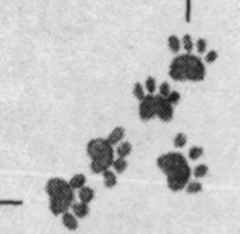

The lobby of the No-Fleas-on-Us Suites was as run down as a caterpillar that forgot to look both ways before crossing the interstate. It was hard to believe a dump like this could live up to its name. Just walking from the front door to the front desk made me as itchy as if I'd rolled around a patch of poison ivy in a cheap wool suit.

I rang the bell and waited.

Finally, a clerk showed up. The tag on his threadbare polyester vest said EDDIE, but his eyes said trouble. Not Trouble with a capital T. More like lowercase trouble.

"I'm looking for Delilah Gorbish," I told him.

"And who are you supposed to be?" he snarled.

"Bud Barkin, Private Eye."

"Yeah, well, I might know something and I might not know something," Eddie said.

In all my years in the detective game, I've been called a lot of things (smart, intelligent, clever, bright, cute, adorable, talented, funny, tough, and as sensitive as a finely tuned concert piano, to name just a few), but one thing I've never been called is stupid. I knew what Eddie was after.

“Maybe this will help jog your memory,” I said, sliding a two-for-one coupon for the Big Slice Pizzeria across the desk. Eddie liked what he saw. He pocketed the coupon and spilled what he knew.

“She’s the dame with the curly blonde ears,” he started off, “and a nervous way of breathing. Sort of like a hummingbird with a bad case of . . .”

“The jitters?” I suggested.

“That’s it,” said Eddie, “the jitters. Well, she was staying here until a little after midnight. That’s when she arrived with a big beefy guy and told me she was checking out. Paid her bill with cash money and took off. That’s the last I seen her.”

Eddie’s eyes got all misty. I sensed we were

heading for a moment when a sensitive soul is revealed beneath a hardened exterior.

"All she left behind was the fresh scent of tropical breezes with a hint of citrus," he went on with a catch in his throat. "You know what she told me? She told me I was impossibly handsome."

"In a cute and puppyish sort of way?"

Eddie looked up. "How'd you know?"

"Let's just say she's broken more than one heart in the past thirty-six hours."

He sniffed back a tear or two. "Dames," he said.

"Dames," I repeated.

We fell silent, a couple of Joes with broken hearts in a sleazy hotel lobby waiting for the twenty-four-hour diner down the street to open up so we could get a cup of cheap coffee to drown our sorrows and get on with our day. There were a million stories like ours in this crazy city. Stories about guys and dames and coffee and teakettles and fish. But that's another story.

"Is that all she left?" I asked Eddie. "The fresh scent of tropical breezes with a hint of citrus?"

"That's all," Eddie said. "No, wait. There was something else. I went to clean her room and found this."

He pulled a box out from under the counter. It was the same box Delilah had shown me in my office earlier—the same, except now it was empty.

"Did she ever talk about this box?" I asked Eddie. "Did she ever tell you what was inside?"

Eddie shook his head. "Sorry, Barkin," he said. "I wish I could help you out, but that's all I know."

I nodded. How much information did I think I could get with one lousy two-for-one coupon, anyway?

"One more thing and I'll leave you to your memories," I told him. "The big beefy fellow Delilah left with. Was there anything you can tell me about him?"

"Let's put it this way," Eddie said. "I wouldn't want to meet up with him in a dark alley on a moonless night."

"That fits a lot of guys," I told him. "Anything special about this one?"

Eddie gave it some thought. "He had a tattoo," he said finally.

"A tattoo?"

"Yeah, a heart with initials inside."

"Do you remember what the initials were?"

"Sure," he told me. "They were C. C. and—"

Eddie stopped speaking and started trembling like a cup of custard on a runaway skateboard at the sight of something behind me. I turned. There in the doorway stood Delilah Gorbish. And with her was none other than Crusty Carmady.

He was holding a teakettle.

Howie's Writing Journal

Writing rocks!!!!!!

I never even saw that one coming!

Hmm, let's see, should Crusty and Delilah be there together, like partners in crime or something, or . . .

CHAPTER 7: "THE TRUTH ABOUT CRUSTY AND DELILAH"

"Let go of me, you big lug!" Delilah said, twisting in Carmady's grip. "You gotta help me, Mr. Barkin. Crusty's no good, I tell you! He's gone as bad as . . ."

"A package of Limburger cheese left open on the backseat of a locked car on a hot summer day?" I suggested.

"Almost," Delilah said with a shudder.

"Shut yer yappers, the two of youse,"

Crusty said. His manner of speaking made me question whether he was really from Iowa. "Barkin, you and your similes always did get on my nerves. I wasn't figurin' on seein' youse here. Lucky for me you *are,* 'cause now I can kill two birds with one stone."

I didn't like the sound of that and I told him so. "Now you listen to me, Carmady, and you listen good. There's going to be no killing in this book, you got me? *Children* are going to be reading this book—*schoolchildren!*"

Carmady turned as pale as a ghost eating a peeled potato in a snowstorm. "I didn't know about the *schoolchildren,*" he said. "I was a schoolchildren once. I wasn't always a bad egg, you gotta believe me, Barkin."

My eyes got all misty. I sensed I was about to play the sap.

"I believe you, Carmady. And you gotta believe me when I tell you that you can be a good egg again. Just let go of the dame and drop the teakettle."

Carmady did like I asked.

Delilah ran across the room and was on me like a piece of lint on a cheap wool suit.

Howie's Writing Journal

Uncle Harold was just reading over my shoulder and pointed out that I used the image of a cheap wool suit before. He said, "You don't want to overuse images, Howie."

He's right.

Delilah ran across the room and was on me like a piece of lint on a finely tuned concert piano. "Oh, thank you," she cried. "Thank you, Mr. Barkin."

If I wasn't a dog, I would have turned redder than a freshly painted fire hydrant.

"You're welcome, sweetheart. I've got just one question."

"What is it?"

"What was in that box? And what's the story with you and Carmady? And who threw the book at the Big Fish? And did you really sing in the choir, and if you did, are you a soprano? And are you really from Iowa? And who do you like more, Eddie or me?"

"That's more than one question," Delilah pointed out.

"Details, details," I muttered.

"Aw, you big galoot," she said, batting her eyelashes in a way that I was pretty sure gave me the answer to my last question at least.

Crusty Carmady cleared his throat. "I'm on the verge of goin' bad again," he said. "Can we get the story back on track?"

"Sorry," I said. "Maybe I should ask you a question first, Carmady. You said you were going to kill two birds with one stone. Assuming I was one bird, what was the other?"

Crusty gave Delilah a ~~look that spelled trouble with a capital~~ nasty look. "Why don't you tell him, sister?"

"Hey," I said, "watch who you call sister."

Delilah shook her head. "It's all right," she

told me. "He called me sister because . . . because I'm his sister."

Except for the sound of Eddie snoring due to being left out of an entire chapter, the lobby of the No-Fleas-on-Us Suites hotel got as quiet as a mime with a bad case of laryngitis.

Howie's Writing Journal

Oh, I'm good!

Who would have thought that Crusty and Delilah were brother and sister?

I wouldn't, that's for sure!

Uncle Harold probably would say that I should have known—and I would have known if I'd outlined—but it's more fun this way. The only problem is that the story doesn't make a whole lot of sense. There are a lot of loose ends.

Okay, let's see.

I'll write down everything I think the reader might be wondering about, then I'll figure out how it all ties together, and then I'll be done.

Writing is so easy, really, when you know what you're doing.

HOWIE'S WRITING JOURNAL

List of loose ends

1. Why did Delilah come from Iowa to find Crusty?
2. Did somebody really give her the box, or did she just make that up?
3. What was in the box and what happened to it?
4. Why did Crusty come back to the hotel with Delilah?

5. What's the other part of Crusty's tattoo? (C. C. + ?)
6. Did Delilah really need Bud Barkin's help in the first place?
7. What does the Big Fish have to do with anything?
8. What did the Big Fish want Bud Barkin to get from Crusty Carmady?
9. Who threw the book through the Big Fish's window?
10. Is the Big Fish okay?
11. Who's going to pay for all those broken windows?

12. Is Delilah a criminal too? (I don't think so, because I think she and Bud Barkin should end up together.)
13. How can I make it so that there's something more to Delilah's character than meets the eye, so the real Delilah won't be mad at me?
14. Does the reader have a clear enough picture of Bud Barkin? (I might need more adjectives.)

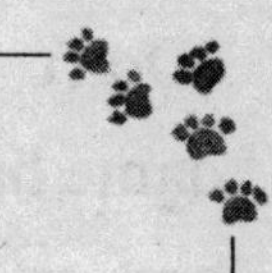

CHAPTER 8: "ALL TIED UP"

"It looks like we've got some loose ends to tie up," I said, breaking the silence.

"I suppose you've got it all figured out," Delilah said, "seeing as how you are the smartest private eye in town, not to mention the most impossibly handsome in a cute and puppyish sort of way."

Eddie woke up and started in crying. "That's what you said *I* was," he whimpered.

I turned and shook him by the shoulders. "Don't waste your tears," I told him. "This dame has more false notes than a badly tuned concert piano."

"There's more to me than meets the eye," Delilah said.

"Don't rush me," I told her. "We've got twelve other loose ends to tie up before we get to that one. Eddie, I want you to place a call for me."

"Anything you say, Bud."

"I want you to call Buttercup, Iowa." Delilah and Crusty gasped. "City Hall, Department of Records."

While Eddie was dialing, I examined the empty box even more carefully than I had in the last chapter when the reader wasn't looking.

"'Property of Miss Lucille's Dance and

Window Glazing Academy, Buttercup, Iowa,'" I read aloud. "I don't suppose this box held *tap shoes* by any chance, did it, Carmady?"

Crusty would have been as speechless as a mime with a bad case of laryngitis if I hadn't already used that simile and couldn't think of another one now. "Oh, you're good, Barkin," he said at last, "but maybe you're not as good as you think you are."

"And maybe I'm better," I told him.

Eddie cleared his throat. "I've got City Hall on the line, Bud."

I took the phone from him. A minute later I had all the answers I needed.

"I want everybody sitting down," I said. "I've got some talking to do, you've got some listening to do, and the reader's got some reading to do, so let's get comfy."

"Really, Inspector," said Crusty Carmady, "what is the meaning of this? I'll have you know I was nowhere near the scene of the crime on the night of the sixteenth. I was at a cricket match with my cousin Reggie. He'll vouch for me. So, as you won't be needing me, I'll just—"

"Button up, Carmady. Don't think you can pull a fast one by slipping into some other kind of mystery novel. I happen to know you're a master of disguise, but you can't fool me. Oh, you had me fooled once. But I'm older now and wiser, not to mention smarter and more intelligent."

Crusty buttoned up.

"The thing of it is, you're not Crusty

Carmady at all, are you? Crusty Carmady is back in Buttercup. You stole his name when you stole those tap shoes from Miss Lucille's and took the first Greyhound west. Your real name is Rusty Macramé. You're wanted in five states for breaking windows. Your accomplice may be your sister, but she's no more Delilah Gorbish than I am. Her name is Mindy Macramé, and the only honest thing she's told me about herself is that she was a straight-A student at Miss Lucille's Dance and Window Glazing Academy. She could have had a future, but that's in the past. Instead, she followed you into a life of crime. You break 'em, she glazes 'em. Nice little racket you two have going. But it's over. You hear me? It's over."

Delilah—I mean Mindy—started to sob. I turned and shook her by the shoulders. "Don't waste your tears," I said. "You lost reader sympathy in the last paragraph."

She raised her chin. "I was trying to go straight, honest I was. I was bringing Rusty back his tap shoes after he got sprung from Sing Sing in the hopes that he'd start dancing again. It's true I was Miss Lucille's star at window glazing, but my brother could tap like nobody's business. Rusty was all of Miss Lucille's dreams wrapped up in one. She's getting on in years now, and I thought, I hoped—"

She didn't get to finish her sentence. The door flew open, and in walked the Big Fish and a couple of his goons.

"We have some unfinished business," he growled. "Barkin, I trust you got what I sent you for."

"Not yet," I told him. I picked up Mindy's purse and removed a brand-new tube of caulking. "This belongs to you, I believe," I said as I handed it over.

The Big Fish smiled and shoved something into my open paw. It was money. Cash money.

"But we was workin' fer *you,*" Rusty Macramé said to the Big Fish.

"*Was* being the key word," said the Big Fish. "I never told you to break any windows. The window glazing operation was to be on the up-and-up. But you just had to have excitement, didn't you? Once a pair of petty criminals, always a pair of petty criminals, that's what I say. Oh, and Mindy?"

"Yes, B. F.?"

"Thank you for returning my book, but the next time I loan you something, kindly return it in a more, shall we say, conventional manner. Of course, where the two of you are going, there really won't be a next time, will there?"

The Big Fish and his goons departed, laughing.

"Eddie," I said, "I'm going to ask you to place one more call for me."

"The police, Bud?"

"The police, Eddie. Ask for Sergeant Pepper. Then once these two have been hauled in, what say you close up here and we go see if that twenty-four-hour diner down the street is open for business? I don't know about you, but I could use a cup of cheap coffee to drown my sorrows and get on with my day."

"Sounds good, Bud."

As Eddie lifted the phone I crossed to the sofa, pulled aside a cushion, and tossed what I found behind it to Rusty Macramé. "The other bird," I said.

"Bud, I've got Sergeant Pepper on the line."

I was reaching for the phone when I heard Rusty say to his sister, "They were too small, anyway." I figured he was talking about the tap shoes I'd just tossed him. But maybe he was talking about his dreams.

THE END

Howie's Writing Journal

Phew! Writing a mystery was hard work! But I really liked Bud Barkin. It was fun being somebody else for a while.

Delilah ended up liking her character too. I guess it helped that she was Mindy Macramé instead of Delilah Gorbish.

Uncle Harold said he liked my writing but that I still had too many loose ends. "How do you explain all the things that don't make sense?" he asked me.

"Red herrings," I told him.

There wasn't a whole lot he could say to that.

I guess maybe if I had outlined first, I wouldn't have had all those loose ends. But then I might never have come up with the Big Fish or Miss Lucille's Dance and Window Glazing Academy or all sorts of other good stuff.

Who knows what I'll come up with in my next book?

Maybe it will even have a pig.

What's next from Howie's overactive imagination? Here's a sample from

The ~~Amazing~~ Odorous Adventures of Stinky Dog

HOWIE'S WRITING JOURNAL

I am so upset I can't write! Well, okay, I can write, but I can't write a book! I owe my editor another book soon, and I don't even have an idea. I don't think my editor would be very happy to get a book about how I just had my third bath in three days!

You would think—what with his being a college professor and her being a lawyer and all—that Mr. and Mrs. Monroe would be smart enough to figure out that a dog isn't a dog without certain smells in his life.

But do they say, "Oh, Howie, what is that delightful aroma—a new aftershave?"

Nooooo. They say, "P. U.! Howie, you stink! Have you been rolling around in the compost heap again? Now you're going to have to have another bath."

Then they tell me that the pile of garbage and rotting food and smelly weeds in the far corner of the yard is there to make fertilizer for their garden. Fine. I have nothing against fertilizer.

In fact, I'm all for fertilizer. But how come they get to enjoy it and Uncle Harold and I don't?

Life is so unfair.

Especially when you're a dog.

I'm going up to Toby's room to sulk. Maybe a good sulk will clear my head so I can come up with an idea for my next book.

Oh, the curse of the writer's life! Readers demand more books. Editors give you contracts, then insist that you actually write the books you promised you would. But what of the poor writer? Is he a machine, churning out books as if they were nothing more than chew bones or squeaky toys? (Not that I have anything against chew bones or squeaky toys.) Or is he a living, breathing creature made of flesh and blood who can't be expected to create when he's been scolded (again) for rolling around in the compost heap and made to suffer the indignity of three baths in three days!?

Life is so unfair.

Especially when you're a dog.

And a writer.